Amelia Bedelia

Road Trip!

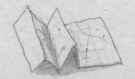

#3

☆ Amelia Bedelia

Road Trip! ☆

by **Herman Parish**

pictures by **Lynne Avril**

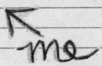

me

 Greenwillow Books
An Imprint of HarperCollins Publishers

Library of Congress Cataloging-in-Publication Data
Parish, Herman.
Amelia Bedelia road trip! / by Herman Parish ; pictures by Lynne Avril.
pages cm.—(Amelia Bedelia chapter books ; #3)
Summary: Fun and fiascoes ensue when young Amelia Bedelia and her parents take
a road trip through their state.
ISBN 978-0-06-209503-9 (trade ed.)—ISBN 978-0-06-209502-2 (pbk ed.)—
ISBN 978-0-06-227057-3 (pob)
[1. Automobile travel--Fiction. 2. Vacations—Fiction. 3. Family life—Fiction. 4. Humorous stories.]
I. Avril, Lynne, (date) illustrator. II. Title. III. Title: Road trip!
PZ7.P2185Aq 2013 [Fic]—dc23 2013013831

16 17 CG/OPM 20 19 18 17 16 15 14   First Edition

 Greenwillow Books

For John & Dennis—

A couple of Romans—H. P.

For Emily, whom I first met at the lake

and who is now casting for the big fish—L. A.

Contents

Chapter 1

Roamin' Holiday

Amelia Bedelia's father came home from work in a great mood. He kissed his wife. He scratched Amelia Bedelia's dog, Finally, in her favorite spot (right behind the ears). Amelia Bedelia was lying on the

HA HA HA

A!

HA

rug next to Finally, doing her homework. Amelia Bedelia's father knelt down next to her, but he didn't kiss her on the head as usual. He started tickling her.

"*Ha-ha-ha-ha!*" she squealed.

He tickled Amelia Bedelia's most ticklish spot, right under her arms.

SSSSSttToopp!

"Stop it!" she shrieked, laughing louder. But he kept right on tickling,

"Mom! Help!" yelled Amelia Bedelia.

Sto

Her mother ran to her rescue. Amelia Bedelia's mom began tickling her dad at *his* most ticklish spot, right under his chin.

He laughed and hollered, "Family

Stop!

tickle, tickle

2

HA HA HA HA!   ha ha ha!

tickle contest!" With one hand still tickling Amelia Bedelia, he tickled his wife right behind her knee, which was *her* worst tickle spot. She began laughing uncontrollably. *"Ah-ha-ha-ha-ha-ha . . ."*

They all collapsed in a heap on the living room floor, laughing and giggling and gasping for breath. Finally raced around them, barking and wagging her tail.

HA! HA! HA

ha ha ha!

HA HA!

tickle, tickle

ckle, tickle

ha ha!

BARK!
BARK!

3

Amelia Bedelia's dad stood up and helped her mom to her feet.

"Well, honey," said Amelia Bedelia's mother. "Thanks for the comic relief. That was a fun homecoming."

"Guess what, guys?" he said. "My boss gave me a bonus week of vacation for doing a good job at work."

"Wow!" said Amelia Bedelia. "Yay, Dad!"

"Congratulations," said her mom. "You certainly earned it. What would you like to do?"

"Well, I was thinking . . . ," said her dad. "How about we all go off to roam?"

"Yippee!" shouted Amelia Bedelia.

"We're going to Rome!"

Amelia Bedelia jumped up from the floor and kept jumping up and down, clapping her hands. She had paid enough attention in geography class to know

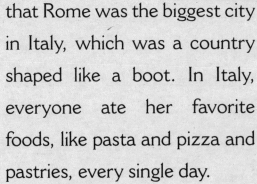

that Rome was the biggest city in Italy, which was a country shaped like a boot. In Italy, everyone ate her favorite foods, like pasta and pizza and pastries, every single day.

Amelia Bedelia hugged her dad. Then she grabbed her mom's

BARK, BARK!

hands and began dancing around the room with her.

Finally barked and barked.

"Golly," said her dad. "I didn't think you would get *that* excited. Haven't you ever been roamin'?"

"How could I be Roman?" asked Amelia Bedelia. "I was born in the United States of America."

Amelia Bedelia's mother stopped dancing but held on to Amelia Bedelia's hands. "Sweetheart," she said, "where do you think we're going?" She had a funny look on her face.

"To Rome, in Italy," said Amelia Bedelia.

"Italy?" said her dad. "We aren't going

to Rome, Italy. We're going to roam . . . around."

"Around?" asked Amelia Bedelia. "Where's around? Around where?"

"Around here," said her dad. "Close to home. For now, we'll have to give Italy the boot." Her dad chuckled as her mother groaned.

Amelia Bedelia was disappointed and her dad's lame joke made her feel worse. She felt like giving him the boot.

"Sorry to let you down, sweetie," said Amelia Bedelia's mom. "If we were going to Rome in Italy, I'd be really excited, too."

"But, Mom," said Amelia Bedelia, "what's Dad even talking about?"

"Don't worry," said her mom. "I'm sure we'll have fun."

Amelia Bedelia's mom made an Italian dinner to cure their disappointment. They had spaghetti and meatballs and crusty bread. They had salad with Italian dressing.

"We'll eat our salads last," said Amelia Bedelia's mom. "Because that's how they do it in Rome."

"Well," said her dad. "When going to roam, do as the Romans do."

"Honey," said Amelia Bedelia's mom, "if you make one more bad joke, you'll roam alone."

After the dishes were done, Amelia Bedelia's father unfolded a road map and spread it out on the dining-room table. He pointed to a spot on the map and said, "We are here."

"I don't see us," said Amelia Bedelia.

"Our house is way too small to show up on this map," said her dad. "This little area is our town. See, right here is Main Street. This tiny green square is the park in front of City Hall."

Looking at the map made Amelia Bedelia feel dizzy. She felt like a bird, flying higher than any other bird, looking

down on everyone and everything.

"I thought it might be fun to just drive around our own state," said her dad. "There are fun places to go and fun things to do right here."

"This will be great!" said her mother. "There's a lot to see in our own backyard."

"What!" said Amelia Bedelia. "First we're not going to Italy, and now we're not even leaving the backyard? What kind of dorky vacation is that?"

Her parents explained that *backyard* could mean *nearby*. They would be traveling hundreds of miles, maybe a thousand miles, before they returned home. That made Amelia Bedelia feel better—and worse.

At bedtime, Amelia Bedelia turned off her light, but she couldn't fall asleep. She was excited about their road trip, and nervous too. She'd never spent a week away from home before, plus she'd miss Finally. She wondered what would happen to them while they were away. What would happen at home that they would miss?

That night, she dreamed all kinds of crazy dreams. When she got up the next morning, she was super tired. Amelia Bedelia felt like she needed a vacation!

Chapter 2

Packing It In

The day they left was bright and sunny. Amelia Bedelia's father was in the driveway, putting their luggage in the car. Amelia Bedelia dragged her bag outside. There were tons of bags piled next to the car—enough luggage for two families!

"Can all of that really fit in our car?" asked Amelia Bedelia.

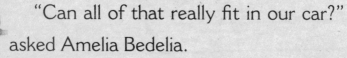

"No problem," said her father. "It's part of the job of being a dad, knowing how to pack a trunk."

"A trunk is definitely too big and heavy," said Amelia Bedelia. "You should use regular bags like Mom and I do." She handed her luggage to him.

"Good thinking," said her father. As he lifted her bag, an electrical plug and cord slipped out and dangled in the air. He set the bag back down. "What have you got in here?"

Amelia Bedelia opened her bag and took out her desk lamp. "You told me to pack light. This is the only light in my room that isn't attached to the ceiling."

"You won't need that," said her dad. "There will be lights where we're going." Then he pointed into her bag. "Is that your backpack?"

"It sure is," said Amelia Bedelia, holding it up for him to see. "You told me to pack my backpack too."

Her father shook his head. "I meant, pack it full of stuff you want to take, not pack it *inside* your suitcase. Where's the checklist I asked you to make?"

Amelia Bedelia reached into her suitcase and pulled out a sheet of paper. It was covered with checkmarks. "Making a list of checks got boring," said Amelia Bedelia, "so I switched sizes and colors to make it more interesting."

Her dad shook his head and said, "Now, hold everything—"

"Hold everything?" said Amelia Bedelia. "Dad, I can't pick up all this stuff!"

"HONEY!" hollered Amelia Bedelia's

father to Amelia Bedelia's mother.

Amelia Bedelia's mother took Amelia Bedelia back inside to help her repack. "Amelia Bedelia," she said. "In most families, dads pack cars and moms ask for directions and kids ask, 'Are we there yet?' You'll see how it works."

When they went back outside, the heap of luggage was neatly packed in the car. Amelia Bedelia handed her bag to her dad.

"Thanks, sugar," he said. "I've got just the spot." He slid it into an empty space. Now the trunk looked like one of those wooden puzzles that are impossible to put back together once you take them apart.

"Run and get Finally, okay?" he said.

"You're not stuffing her in the trunk too, are you?" said Amelia Bedelia.

"Don't be silly," said her dad. "There's no room."

Amelia Bedelia knew her dad was teasing. Finally was going to a kennel called the Paw Palace. They were going to drop her off on their way out of town.

At long last, Amelia Bedelia, her parents, and Finally were ready to leave.

When her dad backed out of the driveway, Amelia Bedelia felt the car go *bump-bump* as they drove over the uneven sidewalk and out into the street. That *bump-bump* feeling always meant that she was home.

It suddenly dawned on Amelia Bedelia that she wouldn't feel that *bump-bump* for a whole week. She was homesick already!

They dropped off Finally at the Paw

Palace. As she got back into the car, Amelia Bedelia wiped her eyes.

"Don't worry," said her mom. "Finally will be fine. She'll get to hang out with other dogs, and your friend Diana is going to take her for walks, right?"

"I know," said Amelia Bedelia. "And my friend Charlie is bringing his dog, Pierre, to visit. Plus, guess what? The Paw Palace even has a puppy pizza night!"

"Hey," said her dad. "The next time I'm in the doghouse, I'm going to check in there."

"You're out of luck, honey," said Amelia Bedelia's mom. "They won't take you unless you're housebroken."

Amelia Bedelia burst out laughing. Even her dad had to laugh. He usually made the jokes in the family. This vacation was switching things around.

"Good one, Mom," said Amelia Bedelia, leaning forward to pat her mom on the shoulder. She glanced at the dashboard.

"Hey," she said. "Why is that little arrow pointing at the letter E?"

Her parents looked at the gas gauge, then at each other. They both blurted out, "Didn't you fill the car with gas?"

"You both can," said Amelia Bedelia. "There's a station right there."

While her dad pumped the gas, Amelia Bedelia and her mother got out to buy a snack. They'd gone barely a mile so far, but they were already hungry. "The fun is about to begin," said Amelia Bedelia's mom. "Look, we're on the edge of town."

Amelia Bedelia looked around for a cliff or ledge, but things seemed pretty flat. She noticed a sign with the name of their town on it. Under the name was the word POP. and the number 1,007.

"Mom, whose Pop is that?" asked Amelia Bedelia, pointing at the sign.

Her mother smiled and said, "That pop isn't someone's father. It's short for 'population.' That number tells you how many people live in our town."

Amelia Bedelia let out a low whistle. She couldn't believe it. Did *that* many people really live where she did? Amelia Bedelia ran back to the car, dug a crayon and her camera out of her backpack, then ran back to the sign. She made an X through the 7 and

wrote the number 4 below, since the three of them would be out of town. Then she took a picture of it. When they returned from their vacation, she would bike over and change it back to 1,007 again.

"Ready to hit the road?" asked Amelia Bedelia's dad. He was fiddling with something on the dashboard.

"There," he said. "I set the odometer to zero so we can tell how many miles we drive." He turned around and waggled his eyebrows at Amelia Bedelia. "If a word ends in '-ometer,' it counts things. The odometer measures our distance. The speedometer measures our speed. What does a thermometer do?"

"It measures temperature to tell how hot or cold things are," said Amelia Bedelia.

"Right!" said her dad. "And who counts how many treats you have each day?"

Amelia Bedelia looked at her mother for help, but her mom just looked back, shook her head, and shrugged her shoulders.

"Give up?" said her dad as he began to chuckle. "That's a mom-ometer!"

Things were back to normal as they drove off on their road trip adventure.

Chapter 3

Neither Here nor There

"Are we there yet?" asked Amelia Bedelia.

Her dad looked back at her in the rearview mirror and said, "That's the best thing about roaming around. Since we don't have a destination, wherever we are, we're already there."

Amelia Bedelia had to think about that for a minute. Then she said, "Well, if we're there, what can I do for fun?"

Her mother reached into her travel bag, pulled out a book, and handed it to her. Amelia Bedelia flipped through it, but there were no comics, puzzles, or stories.

"You should get your money back, Mom," said Amelia Bedelia. "All the pages in this book are blank."

"I know," said her mother. "It's a journal. What's in it is up to you. You can write in it or draw in it or both. It will be your record of our vacation—like a diary." Her mother handed her a brand-new box of colored pencils, too.

"This feels like homework," said Amelia Bedelia.

"It can't be," said her dad. "You're not at home."

She couldn't argue with that.

"It'll be fun," said her mother. "Years from now, you can read it and remember what you were thinking and feeling."

They turned onto a big highway and drove along with lots of other cars. They listened to the radio until the last station faded into static. Then Amelia Bedelia noticed the noise that became the soundtrack of their trip: the hum of tires on the road accompanied by the wind rushing by her window.

Sometimes they passed other cars. Sometimes other cars passed them.

Amelia Bedelia stared at the passengers. Where were they all going? Were they roaming too? A little boy stared back at her, then stuck out his tongue. She laughed and waved. He waved back and laughed too.

Amelia Bedelia gazed at the houses they drove by. What were those people like? Did they have dogs? Did they have kids her age? Would they be friends if she knew them? Did her friends miss her? Did Finally miss her?

Her daydream ended when her dad bellowed, "Adventure, here we come!" as he took the next exit off the interstate. He began singing, "Off we go, into the wild green yonder!" Amelia Bedelia was amazed. Her dad was *so* happy—he always sang the wrong words when he felt goofy.

They had to drive much slower now, because they were on a two-lane road. They drove past old houses and farms

and barns. They drove by cows and sheep. They crossed a bridge and parked.

"We must be there," said Amelia Bedelia.

"Exactly," said her mother. "Lunch will be served on the bank of that stream."

Amelia Bedelia's father grabbed their picnic lunch from the trunk and pulled out a blanket for them to sit on. "This will keep the ants from joining us," he said.

Too bad, thought Amelia Bedelia. She kind of wished that some of her aunts and uncles and cousins had come along to keep her company in the backseat. It was times like this she *really* wished for a brother and *really, really, really* wished for a sister.

After lunch, her mother made an announcement.

"I was up late last night and early this morning packing. I'm taking a nap. Amelia Bedelia, you're in charge!" Then she closed her eyes and put a floppy hat over her face.

Amelia Bedelia buckled herself in.

Her father leaned over and pointed at the map. "We are right here," he said. His finger was on a picture of a tiny picnic table.

"Hey," said Amelia Bedelia. "Why didn't we sit at the table? It would have been better than the ground."

"There was no table," said her father. "That picnic table is just

a symbol. Look in that
little box in the corner of
the map. That's the key."

Amelia Bedelia wondered
if her dad needed a nap too.
A cymbal wasn't anything
like a table. She knew that
because she had tried playing
the cymbals in the school
band. And there was no box
on the map. It was flat. Plus, who needs
a key? You need a key to lock the car. But
you don't unlock a map. You unfold it.

Amelia Bedelia's father started the car
and pulled back out on the road. "Well,
so far, so good!" he said.

"Not really," said Amelia Bedelia. "We

haven't gone so far, and it hasn't been so good."

"Ha-ha!" came a laugh from under the floppy hat.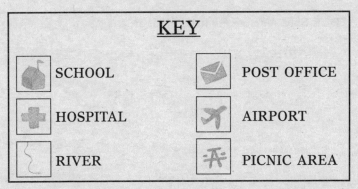

Amelia Bedelia looked at the map again. The road they were on went through a green patch. She looked up and saw trees on both sides of the car.

She noticed a square in the corner of the map, filled with tiny pictures. A school had a little flag on top, just like her school did. A hospital was a red cross. A little envelope was a post office. A plane was

KEY

	SCHOOL		POST OFFICE
	HOSPITAL		AIRPORT
	RIVER		PICNIC AREA

an airport. Then she found
each picture on the map itself.

"Maps are fun to figure out,"
said Amelia Bedelia.

"I'm glad you think so," said
her father. "Do you see where we are?"

Amelia Bedelia put her finger on the
map. "Yup," she said. "I've got us."

"Great. Can you figure out how to get us
to Route Twenty-three?" he asked.

Amelia Bedelia looked at the map.
She turned it sideways, then upside
down, then right side up again. To prove
that she was thinking, she let out a giant
"*Hmmmmmmm.*"

Hmmmm

At last she shouted, "I've got it! Keep going straight, then turn left onto this blue squiggly road, and it'll take you there."

"*Hmmmmmmm,*" said her father. He looked at Amelia Bedelia in the rearview mirror. "A blue squiggly line is usually a river."

river

Sure enough, next to the blue squiggle picture was the word "river." She was about to apologize when she noticed something about the road they were on.

"Dad," said Amelia Bedelia, "what does it mean when the solid black line for the road changes into a brown line

"Snorp!"

with dashes?" She looked up as they passed a sign that read PAVEMENT ENDS.

"Dirt road!" bellowed her dad as they skidded a bit on gravel, raising an enormous cloud of dust.

"*Snorp—yewwww!*"

Amelia Bedelia giggled at the sound of her mother snoring.

Her dad smiled and said, "I can't believe she can sleep through this."

They bounced along until they came to a stop sign. The road they were on ended, and another sign gave them a choice. They could turn left or right.

"This isn't on the map," said Amelia Bedelia. "Which way should we go?"

"I have no idea," said her father.

"I vote for left," said Amelia Bedelia.

"I'm thinking right," said her father.

"Call it," said a voice under the hat.

"Heads!" shouted Amelia Bedelia.

"Tails!" shouted her father.

Amelia Bedelia's mother was wide awake now. She could always be counted on to make a decision. She pushed back her hat and flipped a coin in the air. She looked at both of them and then lifted her hand to reveal the winner.

"Tails it is," she said.

They turned right, and away they went, to whatever might come next.

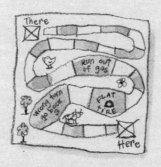

Chapter 4

To Get There, Go Backward

As it turned out, right was wrong. They drove along for what seemed like hours. There were no more signs. There were no other roads to turn down. There were no houses. There was not one person to ask where they were. Just trees and grass and more grass and more trees.

"Now this," said Amelia Bedelia's father, "is what I call roaming."

"And you," said Amelia Bedelia's mother, "are a regular Daniel Boone."

"Daniel who?" asked Amelia Bedelia.

"Daniel Boone was a famous explorer," said her dad. "He wore a coonskin hat while blazing trails across America."

"He sounds cool," said Amelia Bedelia. "Did all that blazing start forest fires?"

"Just campfires," said her mom. "Look him up when we get home—now *that's* official homework, my dear!"

Amelia Bedelia got out her journal. She drew a picture of Daniel Boone. She drew a picture of a bumpy road. She drew

ants on a blanket. She drew her lunch. She drew her own map key for important stuff she would like to find.

Amelia Bedelia's father shook his head. "Man," he said, "I have no idea where we are."

"I know," said Amelia Bedelia's mother. "We're in the middle of nowhere."

"Well," said her dad, "if this isn't the middle of nowhere, I'm sure we could see nowhere from here."

As their car climbed the crest of a hill, Amelia Bedelia spied a farmer in his field and shouted, "A human being!"

"Honey, let's ask him where we are," said Amelia Bedelia's mother. Amelia Bedelia's father stopped the car, and her

why

Daniel Boone

very bumpy road!!!

yum!

Ants

my lunc !!!

Map Key

ice cream stand

toy store

any place that sells french fries

cool clothes store

swiming pool

sticker store

bike shop

candy store

amelia bedelia

skateboard park

mother lowered her window.

"Excuse me, sir," said Amelia Bedelia's mother. "We're lost."

"I know," said the farmer. "The only reason anyone drives by here is 'cause they aren't where they're supposed to be."

Amelia Bedelia's mom handed the map to the farmer and pointed to a town. "Can you tell us how to get there?"

The farmer squinted and shrugged. "Sorry, lady, you can't get there from here."

Amelia Bedelia's father laughed, but not like when something is funny.

Her mother didn't know what to say, but Amelia Bedelia did. She leaned forward between the seats and asked, "Mister farmer, sir, if we were already

there, how would we get back here?"

This time, the *farmer* laughed—a real laugh. "Well, little lady, that is a mighty interesting question." Without looking at the map, he began reeling off directions.

Her parents nodded politely as he described signs and landmarks and twists and turns.

"So, that brings you

to right here, folks," the farmer finally said. "'Scuse me now, I've got to get my cows up to the barn for milking."

As he waved good-bye over his shoulder, he called out, "Come on, ladies!" A herd of cows trailed after him, the bells on their necks clanging.

Amelia Bedelia's parents looked at the cows and then at each other. "Did you catch any of that?" asked her dad.

"Not one word," said her mom.

"I did," said Amelia Bedelia, handing them her journal. "I wrote it all down. If we go backward, starting at the top and changing lefts to rights, we'll get to the town."

48

Amelia Bedelia's parents were silent. The truth was, they were dumbstruck.

"It's okay," Amelia Bedelia said. "I'll read the directions to you. First go straight for two miles, passing by a swamp. Turn left at the rock that looks like a teapot, drive three miles, cross a railroad track, turn right, drive for eight more miles . . ." Amelia Bedelia was looking at her journal, so she missed her parents gazing at her with pride.

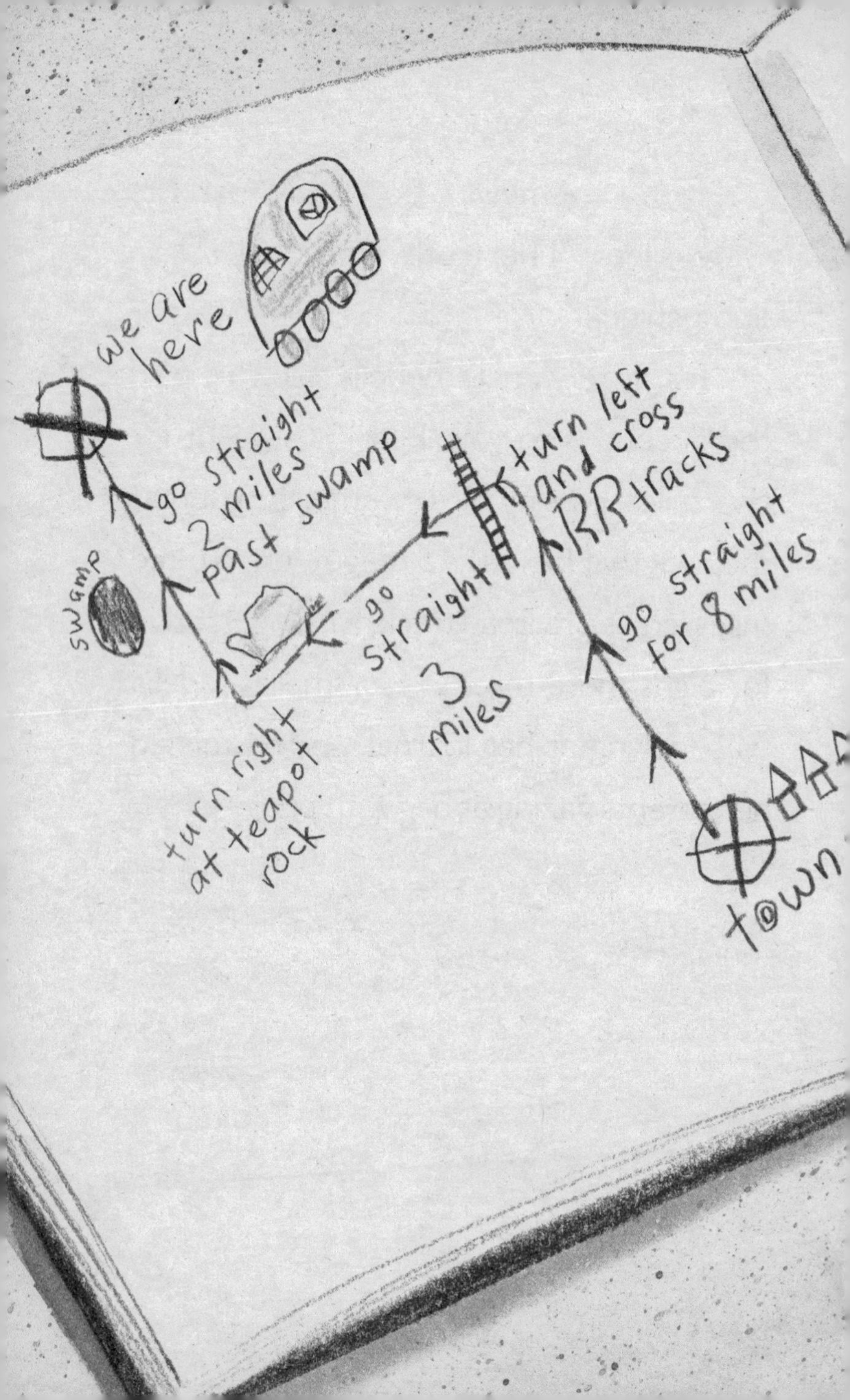

we are here

go straight 2 miles past swamp

swamp

turn right at teapot rock

go straight 3 miles

turn left and cross RR tracks

go straight for 8 miles

town

"Amelia Bedelia," said her mom. "I think you'll find your way in the world, no problem."

"Yup," said her dad. "No doubt about that. You're a regular Danielle Boone!"

He began driving, following Amelia Bedelia's directions word for word.

By the time they got to the little town on the map, it was almost dark. They checked into a motel, then went out for Chinese food. The best part of their meal was the fortune cookies. Amelia Bedelia read her fortune out loud.

"'Learn to fish and you will never go hungry,'" she said.

Then Amelia Bedelia's mother read

51

A journey of a thousand miles begins with a single step.

hers. "'A journey of a thousand miles begins with a single step.'" She took a bite of her cookie, then said, "I'm glad we aren't walking. I feel like we drove nine hundred ninety-nine miles just today. What does yours say, honey?"

Her father leaned back, cleared his throat, and read, "'So far, so bad.'"

Amelia Bedelia was amazed. Then he looked up and smiled.

"You made that up!" she said.

"I sure did," he said. "Just like I'm making up this vacation. Sorry today wasn't any fun. I'll plan things better for tomorrow."

"Awww, Dad," said Amelia Bedelia. "It wasn't that bad."

"And we're together," said her mom.
"That's worth a fortune."

"FAMILY HUG!" yelled Amelia Bedelia.

And the three of them hugged right there in the restaurant. As they left, Amelia Bedelia swept their paper fortunes into her pocket. That night she wrote an entry in her journal. She signed her name

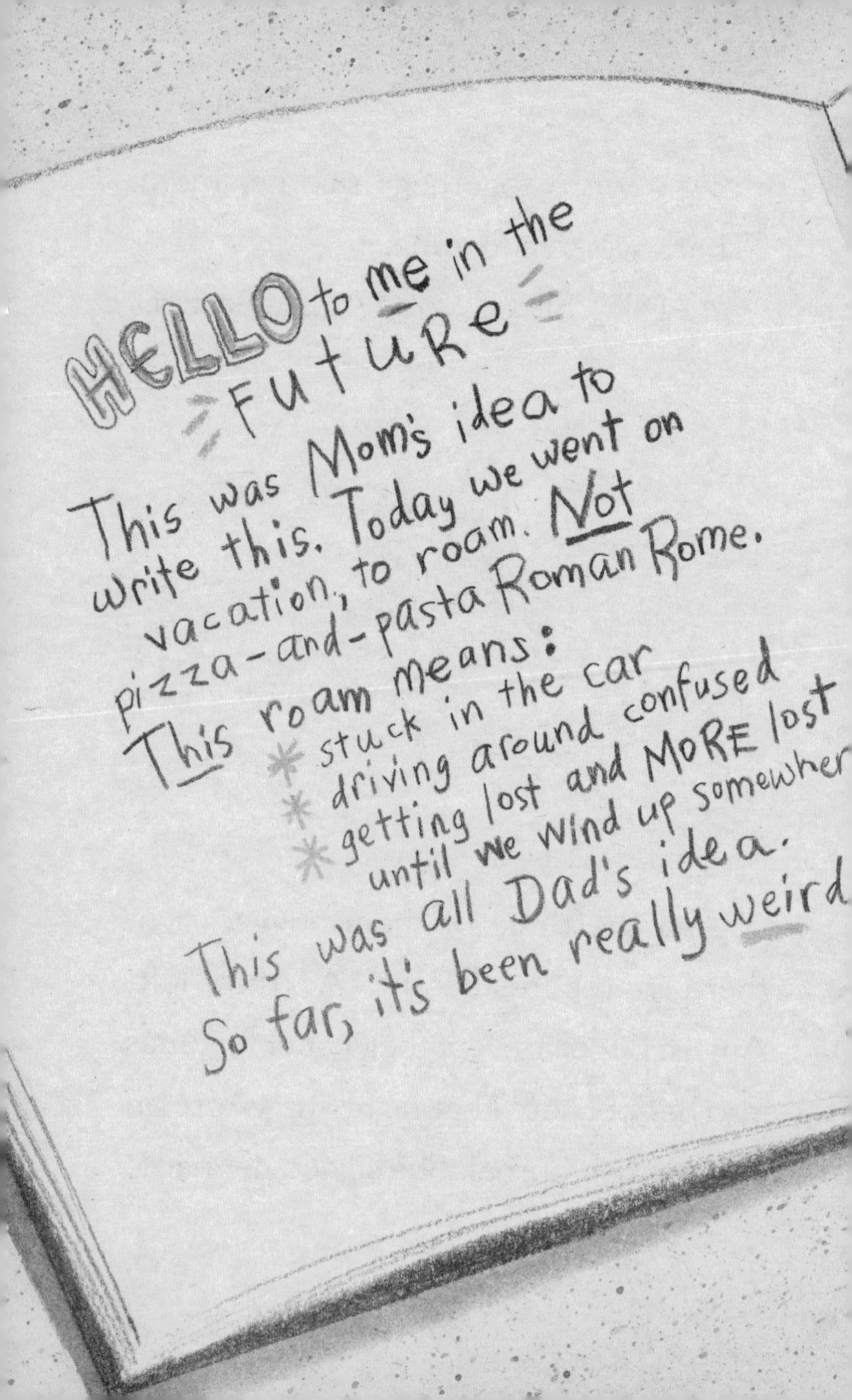

HELLO to me in the FUTURE

This was Mom's idea to write this. Today we went on vacation, to roam. <u>Not</u> pizza-and-pasta Roman Rome.

<u>This</u> roam means:
* stuck in the car
* driving around confused
* getting lost and MoRE lost until we wind up somewhere

This was all Dad's idea. So far, it's been really weird

with the date, to make it official, and she taped her mom's thousand-mile fortune on the first page. Then she read her dad's fortune. What it

really said was FOLLOW YOUR DREAMS. That made her feel terrible about what she had just written. Her father's dream had been to go roaming, but things hadn't gone very smoothly. She promised to be nicer to him tomorrow. Everyone needs a dream, she decided, especially the people you love. She tucked her fortune and her dad's fortune into her journal for later.

Follow your dreams,

Chapter 5

One-Horse Town

The next morning, Amelia Bedelia's father was humming at breakfast. "Good news," he said. "The motel manager told me about a tiny town not far from here. It's historic, with lots of shops, good restaurants, and interesting things to see and do. Best of all, the town is celebrating its three-hundredth birthday, so let's head straight there."

They arrived in no
time and promptly got
lost. Various streets
were closed off with detours.
Amelia Bedelia was certain that her
dad was driving in a circle.

"This sure is a one-horse town," said
Amelia Bedelia's father.

People in fancy costumes wearing

powdered wigs mingled on the sidewalks with people dressed as soldiers from a long time ago. There were real soldiers from today and regular people too. Amelia Bedelia spotted a marching band heading down one street, but she didn't see that one horse in town.

"I'll bet there's a parade or something," said Amelia Bedelia's mother. "Honey, let's ask for directions."

Amelia Bedelia's father shook his head. "Some of these people are from hundreds of years ago. They wouldn't know where things are today."

"Oh, Daddy!" Amelia Bedelia laughed.

"Then I will ask," said her mother.

Before she could, her father headed

down an alley. "At last!" he said. "An open street." He turned onto it and wound up between a drum-and-bugle corps and about thirty girls waving flags and tossing batons into the air.

Spectators on the sidewalks were waving at them. Amelia Bedelia waved back. "What friendly people!" she said.

Amelia Bedelia's mother turned to her father. "Congratulations, honey," she said. "You crashed a parade."

"Crashed?" said Amelia Bedelia. "Did we hit anyone?"

"Not yet," said her mother. "But the day is young."

Amelia Bedelia looked out their back window. Sure enough, they were driving in the middle of a parade. They drove by cheering crowds, under bunting, and past popcorn carts while the drum-and-bugle corps played "Yankee Doodle Dandy."

Finally the parade halted at a grand-stand. Three boys wearing old-timey clothes opened their car doors and escorted Amelia Bedelia and her parents to a stage.

A man who Amelia Bedelia thought must be the mayor shook their hands. "On

behalf of our fair hamlet, we welcome you as our one-millionth visitor. Here is the key to the town." The man bowed and handed Amelia Bedelia a giant key.

"You better keep your key, sir," said Amelia Bedelia. "We can't come back tonight to lock up your town." Then she turned to her father and said, "You were right, Daddy. This *is* a one-horse town."

The smile on the mayor's face faded, while her father's face got very red.

Amelia Bedelia pointed across the square at a statue of a soldier on horseback. "Is that the horse you meant?" she asked.

"That's Major Andrew McClary, our town's founder,"

said the mayor, beaming again. "I'm glad you gave your daughter a lesson in our history. Are you from around here?"

"We *are* right here," said Amelia Bedelia.

"Actually," said Amelia Bedelia's father, "we're on vacation, traveling off the beaten path."

"So far, the path has beaten us," added Amelia Bedelia's mother.

"Well," said the mayor, "if you won't accept this key, at least accept the key to my cabin up on Lake Largemouth."

"Oh, thank you, but we couldn't do that," said Amelia Bedelia's mother.

"Why not?" asked Amelia Bedelia.

Amelia Bedelia's father smiled and nodded, raising his eyebrows.

"I'll convince you at our Founder's Day picnic," said the mayor. "Come on—let's eat!"

They had a terrific time at the picnic. Amelia Bedelia ate cornbread, sausage, apple pie, and 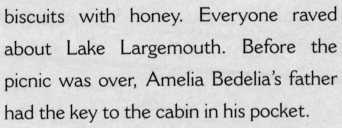 biscuits with honey. Everyone raved about Lake Largemouth. Before the picnic was over, Amelia Bedelia's father had the key to the cabin in his pocket.

"Enjoy yourselves," said the mayor.  "Now listen, if you run into any problems, there's a doc next door."

"Is that where you tie up your boat?" asked Amelia Bedelia.

"No, I've got my own dock," said the mayor. "Dr. Piltin is my neighbor up at the lake. But, really, the only thing you can get sick of up there is relaxing. All the faucets leak, so if you don't mind a *drip-drip-drip* at night, you'll sleep better than you ever have."

"Sold!" said Amelia Bedelia's mother.

Chapter 6

Fish Story

Lake Largemouth was not close, but it sounded like so much fun that the miles seemed to melt away. Amelia Bedelia found the lake on the map. It had tiny symbols of a fish and a boat on it.

"Hey," she said, "These pictures mean that we can go boating and fishing. That fish is as big as the boat. Maybe my fortune

could come true!"

"When I was your age," said her father, "I caught a really big fish." He took one hand off the steering wheel and held it out to show her the size.

Amelia Bedelia's mother shook her head. "When I met your father, that fish was half that size. It's grown bigger every time he talks about it."

Amelia Bedelia's mother had tried to go fishing once too, but she couldn't bear to kill a poor worm just to catch a fish. That made sense to Amelia Bedelia.

Amelia Bedelia's mom and dad started telling funny stories about their summer vacations when they were growing up. Before Amelia

Bedelia knew it, they had arrived.

"Hey, Dad!" yelled Amelia Bedelia. "Was the fish you caught *that* big?"

Her parents' mouths dropped open in awe. Dead ahead was a largemouth bass as big as a semitrailer. It was made of concrete and painted to look like a real fish with scales and everything. It could have swallowed their car.

"Wow," said Amelia Bedelia's mom. "That's how big your dad's fish will be if he keeps telling that story."

"Ha, ha," said Amelia Bedelia's father. He wasn't really laughing, but he sure was

smiling. He parked next to a grocery store.

"Let's go buy some staples," he said.

Staples? wondered Amelia Bedelia. Why did they need staples on vacation? Had he packed a stapler for paperwork?

This was a general store, cozy and chock-full of interesting stuff. Amelia Bedelia walked across the creaky wooden floor to pick out

Greetings from LAKE LARGEMOUTH

It looks like Italy, but made of WATER!

postcards, while her parents shopped.

When it was time to pay, she asked, "Where are the staples?"

"Right here," said her father, waving his hand over eggs, bread, milk, butter, coffee, tea, and sugar.

Amelia Bedelia hoped that her father could relax so he wouldn't mistake food for office supplies.

While her parents enjoyed a cup of coffee, Amelia Bedelia sat in a big rocker on the store's porch and wrote to her friends.

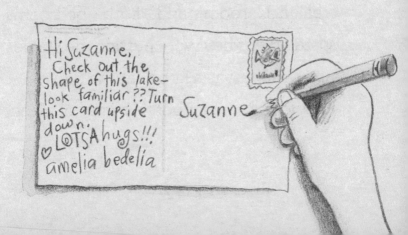

Hi Suzanne,
Check out the shape of this lake— look familiar?? Turn this card upside down.
♡ LOTSA hugs!!!
amelia bedelia

Suzanne

Chapter 7

~~A~~ G~~oo~~d Sport
(Great)

It was love at first sight. Amelia Bedelia thought the cabin was possibly the cutest cabin in the world. It was by the water, so they got a view of the lake from the breakfast room and both bedrooms upstairs. As they were putting the staples away, there was a knock at the door.

"Howdy, neighbor," came a deep,

friendly voice. "I've been expecting you. Stan Piltin's my name, but everyone calls me Doc."

Amelia Bedelia's parents introduced themselves and Amelia Bedelia.

"I am glad to meet you, young lady," said Doc. "My granddaughter Audrey is visiting us. She may be a bit older than you are, but I'm sure you two will get along. She's a good sport."

"Which one?" asked Amelia Bedelia. "Soccer? Basketball?"

Doc laughed. "Actually, it's fishing," he said.

"I need to learn how to fish," said Amelia Bedelia.

"I bet Audrey would be happy to teach you," said Doc. "You just missed her, though. She's out in the boat. In fact, she's fishing right around that bend." He pointed to where the shore of the lake curved around.

"How about we take the mayor's boat for a spin?" said Amelia Bedelia's father. "We can go say hello."

"Great idea," said Doc. "Come with

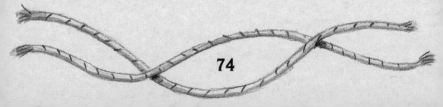

me, and I'll show you the ropes."

"Thanks. I grew up around boats," said Amelia Bedelia's father, "but I'd appreciate the help."

They all went down to their dock and climbed aboard the speedboat tied up there. Everyone put on life jackets. Amelia Bedelia's father got behind the wheel and started the engine. Doc warned them about a big stump

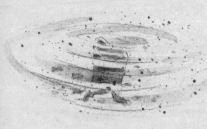

that was submerged about fifty yards off the dock.

"You can't always see it," he said. "Be careful. It snapped the propeller off a boat last summer."

"Thanks for the heads-up," said Amelia Bedelia's father.

As Doc cast them off, he hollered over the roar of the engine. "Amelia Bedelia— find Audrey! You can try something new and get your feet wet!"

"Excuse me?" yelled Amelia Bedelia. Why would Doc want her to get wet feet?

Doc's reply was lost in the roar of the motor. And Amelia Bedelia forgot all about wet feet as her dad steered carefully around the big stump. As she looked down into the clear water, she could see the stump. *Wait*, she thought. Had something big moved down there? Or were her eyes playing tricks on her, just like her ears?

Soon her dad was speeding across Lake Largemouth. Amelia Bedelia liked the cushions on the seats and the shiny brass instruments on the dashboard.

"Do boats work like cars?" she asked.

"Of course not," said her father. "We're on the water."

"That's good," said Amelia Bedelia. "Because this boat has one of those little windows with an arrow pointing at the letter E, just like our car."

Amelia Bedelia's parents looked at the gas gauge, then at each other. Their eyes practically popped out of their heads. "Not again!" they yelled together.

"Steer closer to land," advised Amelia Bedelia's mother. "If we run out of gas, we can swim for it."

"Aye-aye, captain," said her father. He turned hard, swooping as close to shore as he could without running aground. The engine made a sputtering, coughing, wheezing sound, and then . . . silence.

"What boat did you grow up around— the *Titanic*?" asked Amelia Bedelia's mom. "Too bad you didn't grow up around a gas pump too. Now what are we going to do?"

"Fear not," said Amelia Bedelia's father, picking up a boat hook with a long wooden shaft. "It's shallow enough to use this pole to push us around that spit of land. Maybe we'll find someone with gas to spare."

Amelia Bedelia and her mother moved to the stern to stay out of his way as he began pushing them along.

"I know," he said. "Imagine you're in Venice, Italy. I'm your handsome gondolier."

Amelia Bedelia's mother looked at her, then rolled her eyes.

Amelia Bedelia's father tied a handkerchief around his neck.

"Romantico, no?" he asked.

"No!" said her mother.

"Um . . . maybe embarrassing?"
said Amelia Bedelia.

"This will help," he said, clearing his

throat and singing, *"Mi-mi-mi-mi!"* Then, with the fakest Italian accent ever, he launched into "O Sole Mio" (which just happened to be one of Amelia Bedelia's favorite songs), but with new lyrics he made up on the spot.

"O sole mio, please serve me pasta,
With extra sauce and a ton of cheese.
Then bring me a plate of pastries,
With an espresso as strong as me!"

"Bravo, honey," said Amelia Bedelia's mother, laughing.

Amelia Bedelia and her mother clapped loudly, hoping he would stop, but it only encouraged him. Amelia Bedelia's father began singing every Italian word he knew, making up a song that made no sense.

"Buon giorno, gelato . . .
Arrivederci, lasagna . . ."

With a giant shove, he pushed their boat around the bend and sang,

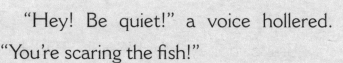

"Ciao, minestrone . . ."

"Hey! Be quiet!" a voice hollered. "You're scaring the fish!"

The voice belonged to a girl sitting in a boat and fishing.

"Hi, Audrey!" Amelia Bedelia hollered back.

"How did you know my name?" asked Audrey.

As they drew nearer, they explained who they were. Audrey blushed. "Sorry I criticized your singing," she said. "All I can think about is catching a big fish. I want to win the Lake Largemouth fishing contest."

"I've never even been fishing," said Amelia Bedelia.

"I can show you how," said Audrey.

"Can I hang out with Audrey?" asked

Amelia Bedelia. "She could teach me how to fish."

"Well, maybe for a bit," said Amelia Bedelia's mother.

"If you can spare some gas, we'll head back," said Amelia Bedelia's father.

"Sure," said Audrey. "Come on over, Amelia Bedelia."

Amelia Bedelia's father used the boat hook to pull their boat right next to Audrey's. Amelia Bedelia stood up and started to step across. Just then, a gust of wind blew the boats apart. Amelia Bedelia had one foot on each boat! She was doing a giant split as the boats drifted farther and farther away from each other.

"Whoaaaaaa!" cried Amelia Bedelia,

waving her arms around to keep her
balance. But it was no use—

SPLUL—LASSSSHHHHH!

Amelia Bedelia bobbed to the surface.
She grabbed the side of Audrey's
boat, and Audrey hauled her in like
a big fish.

SPLUL-LASSSHHH

"Amelia Bedelia!" yelled her father.

"Sweetie!" yelled her mother.

Her parents were frantic until they heard her laughing and sputtering.

Then Amelia Bedelia did what her dog Finally did when she got wet. She shook herself all over, spraying Audrey with water. Now both girls were laughing, and so were Amelia Bedelia's parents.

"Don't worry," said Amelia Bedelia. "The sun is drying me off."

"We'll be fine," said Audrey. "Tell Grandpa Doc to light the grill. We'll be back in an hour with a mess of fish for dinner."

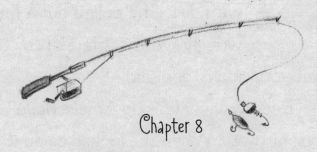

Chapter 8

Hook, Line, and Stinker

Audrey showed Amelia Bedelia her fishing rod and explained all the parts.

"I didn't know fishing was so complicated," said Amelia Bedelia.

"My rod is pretty fancy," said Audrey, "but I always bring along this pole with just a line, a hook, and a bobber. It's really fun to use." As she was talking, Audrey

reached into an old can filled with dirt. She pulled out a fat, wriggly worm. "Here's how to bait your hook," she said.

"Eeee-*yewwww!*" said Amelia Bedelia, looking away. When she looked back, the worm was on the hook. Amelia Bedelia stared at it and said, "Sorry!"

Audrey swung the line with the hook and bobber into the water with a *plop*, then handed the pole to Amelia Bedelia. Amelia Bedelia perched on a cushion, where she could fish and dry off too.

"What kind of fish do you think I'll catch?" asked Amelia Bedelia.

"Any kind," said Audrey. "Maybe catfish, walleye, sunfish, rainbow trout . . ."

Amelia Bedelia was wondering if she would ever figure out fishing when she felt a tug and her bobber vanished under the water.

"You got one!" shouted Audrey.

"What do I do?" said Amelia Bedelia.

"Pull him in!" yelled Audrey.

Amelia Bedelia lifted her pole, and a fish was at the end of her line! It swung back

and forth, above them, around them, and between them, until it hit Amelia Bedelia in the chest. She grabbed it with her free hand. "Gotcha," she said.

"Nice fish," said Audrey. "You've got a good perch there."

"It's very comfortable," said Amelia Bedelia as she sat back down on the cushion while Audrey unhooked her fish.

An hour flew by as Amelia Bedelia caught fish after fish. Audrey was so busy

taking fish off her hook and putting on fresh worms that she barely had a chance to fish herself. But she did tell Amelia Bedelia all kinds of interesting things about fish and how they like to hide in shady spots and near roots and rocks and how she once saw five big trout jump way out of the water at the exact same time.

When they got back to the dock, Doc was waiting for them. "I'm so sorry," he said. "Your parents told me you all ran out of gas. I should have checked. I could kick myself."

"That might hurt,"

said Amelia Bedelia. "I can't kick myself, and I wouldn't even if I could. And neither should you."

Doc's laughter turned into a whistle when Audrey held up the string of fish Amelia Bedelia had caught. "Wow," he said. "Now that's what I call getting your feet wet."

"All of me got wet," said Amelia Bedelia. "I fell in and got soaked."

"That's a good nickname for you," said Audrey. "I'm going to call you Soaky."

"Maybe that's the secret to your beginner's luck," said Doc. "Fishermen are very superstitious—right, Audrey?"

Audrey nodded. "That's why I wear Grandpa's lucky fishing shirt."

"Never wash it," said Doc. "All that luck will go right down the drain."

Amelia Bedelia had been puzzled by Audrey's shirt. It was super old and pretty stinky. Amelia Bedelia pinched her nose and said, "*Pee-yew*! If I'm Soaky, then you're Stinky!"

Audrey laughed. "Deal," she said. She held out her hand, and they shook on it.

Things got a whole lot stinkier when Doc showed Amelia Bedelia how to clean her fish. She was expecting soap and hot water. Instead, he used a knife to scrape off the scales, cut off the heads and tails, and scoop out the insides.

Amelia Bedelia looked queasy.

Audrey grinned. "Do you have the

guts to try it yourself?" she asked.

Amelia Bedelia surveyed the growing mound of fish guts and declared, "There are *plenty* of guts around here!"

Then she cleaned the rest of the fish herself, with advice from Doc. When she had finished, Amelia Bedelia said, "Audrey, now I know why you called this a mess of fish. This is disgusting!"

Chapter 9

Miss Bigmouth

Doc's wife came outside and introduced herself to Amelia Bedelia. "My name is Darlene," she said. "But everyone calls me Mrs. Doc."

"Hi, Mrs. Doc," said Amelia Bedelia. She liked that name. It suited her.

"I invited your parents over for a fish fry," said Mrs. Doc. "So I'm glad you did

your part and supplied the fish."

Mrs. Doc put a huge cast-iron frying pan on the grill. Then she set up a fish-frying assembly line with the girls. Amelia Bedelia took a piece of fish and rolled it in flour with a bit of salt and pepper, then handed it to Audrey, who dipped it in a bowl of egg and covered it with bread crumbs. Then Mrs. Doc slid it into the pan, where it sizzled until it was golden brown.

As the last pieces of fish went in the pan, Amelia Bedelia's parents arrived.

"What a lovely surprise," said Mrs. Doc. "I'm tickled pink that you are here at the lake."

"Don't say 'tickle' near my dad," warned

96

Amelia Bedelia. "He might do it."

Fortunately, her father had his hands full. He was carrying a salad, while her mother had brought her easy-breezy-appetizer-that-everyone-raves-about-but-takes-no-work-at-all. Mrs. Doc took one bite and said, "This is awful good!"

Awful good? thought Amelia Bedelia. *Does she think it's awful or good? It can't be both, can it?*

"You've got to give me this recipe before you leave," said Mrs. Doc. "It's really so yummy!"

"We'll probably take off on Saturday," said Amelia Bedelia's father. "So we can have a day to get back to normal."

"Impossible!" said Doc. "You can't

leave Saturday. That's the day of the fishing contest and the crowning of Miss Bigmouth."

Amelia Bedelia could not believe her ears. You could get a crown for having a big mouth?

"I know a bunch of girls in my class who could be Miss Bigmouth," she blurted out. "They can't keep a secret for five seconds before they blab it to everyone. How do they decide which girl has the biggest mouth?"

"Young lady!" said Amelia Bedelia's mother. "Don't be rude!"

But Doc and Mrs. Doc couldn't stop laughing. "Amelia Bedelia," said Doc, "we're so glad to have you next door,

even for just a few more days!"

"The big mouth isn't on a girl," Audrey explained. "It's on a fish, a bass. Some people call it a largemouth or a widemouth. These days, they usually just call it a bigmouth."

"Sounds like an excuse for a beauty contest," said Amelia Bedelia's mother. She didn't look one bit pleased. "We don't need to stay for that."

"Oh, it's a big honor in these parts," said Doc.

"And skill is involved in the fishing. If it was easy, they would call it 'catching' instead of 'fishing.' Whoever lands the biggest bigmouth wins five hundred dollars."

Amelia Bedelia's mother tilted her head. "The winner of the fishing contest could be a man *or* a woman, right?" she asked. "Has Miss Bigmouth ever caught the biggest fish?"

"Not yet, but maybe she will this year," said Doc.

"I'm going to win," said Audrey. "That's why I've been practicing every

Learn to fish and you will never go hungry.
How to Put a worm on a Hook:
Step 1
Step 2
Step 3
GROSS!!!

day. And I'm counting on having Amelia Bedelia in my boat to bring me luck."

"Speaking of fish," said Mrs. Doc, "supper is on!"

That night Amelia Bedelia worked on her journal before going to sleep. She had lots to write about. She taped her fortune on a blank page.

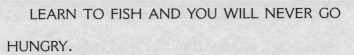

LEARN TO FISH AND YOU WILL NEVER GO HUNGRY.

She decided that if she had an older sister (which she knew was pretty much impossible), she'd like her to be like Audrey. Would Audrey like a younger sister just like her? And what was Audrey going to do with her five hundred dollars?

Chapter 10

Life at the Lake

Amelia Bedelia and her parents adored the cabin. Every day her dad talked about hopping in the car and roaming around, but there were so many fun things to do right where they were!

Amelia Bedelia spent most of every day in the boat with Audrey. The good thing about fishing is that it leaves plenty of time for talking. They talked about school and friends and parents. They talked about movies and TV shows and books and animals. The biggest difference between them was that Audrey had a cat and Amelia Bedelia had a dog. And Audrey was older. But that didn't seem to matter at all. Talking about Finally made Amelia Bedelia miss her, so she wrote a postcard to Diana.

Hi Diana,
Thanks SOOOOooo much for walking Finally. I miss her SOoOOO much! Today I saw a dog with REALLY long hair. They said it was a rushin' wolf hound, but he was in no hurry.
ZZzzz Hug Finally for me!
amelia bedelia

Dad and Mom's
VACATION
SCHEDULE

9:00 Wake up.

9:30 Breakfast

10:00 Dad fishes with Doc.
Mom walks with Mrs. Doc.
I fish with Audrey.

12:00 Lunch

12:45 Nap

2:00 Ride bikes

3:00 Get ice cream!
Try new flavor each day.
Dad's favorite! REally ROcky ROAd
with walnuts the
My favorite size of boulders!
Double Chocolate   Mom's favorite
Cookie Dough
Crunch   Triple Berry Smash

3:30 Read
4:30 (~~aproximut~~) (approximate)
ANoTHER nap

6:00 DINNER
7:30 Go to town.
Hear live music.
(beats dead music!)
9:30 Write in journal
(like I'm doing now)
10:00 Mom or Dad reads me
to sleep.

Chapter 11

Fishing Versus Catching

By Friday, the day before the Bigmouth Festival, the town was filling up with fishing fanatics. Amelia Bedelia and her parents took a walk to the public dock to check out where the fish would be weighed and measured.

Amelia Bedelia and Audrey went fishing later that morning. Audrey practiced casting with her rod and reel while Amelia Bedelia practiced with the cane pole.

Amelia Bedelia knew her dad would admire how organized Audrey was. She was a planner, with a checklist for everything she needed or might need. Her tackle box was filled with lures and spare reels. Audrey even had a strategy.

"You know what, Soaky?" she told Amelia Bedelia. "I'm not going to fish until late in the day. I know where the big fish like to hide. I don't want people to see my fish and try my spot, because then I might not win. I'm going to come in with a huge fish right at the end of the contest, at five o'clock. It's my best shot."

That night, Amelia Bedelia and her

parents and Doc, Mrs. Doc, and Audrey went into town for pizza. It was Amelia Bedelia's dad's idea.

"He's jealous," Amelia Bedelia's mom announced as they studied their menus. "He remembered that tonight our dog is getting pizza at the kennel, so he got a craving for it."

"Puppy pizza day!" said Audrey. "Sweet!"

Amelia Bedelia wondered what Finally would order, as her parents and Mr. and Mrs. Doc tried to outdo one another with how many weird toppings they could put on a pizza. They added olives, peppers, mushrooms, sausage, meatballs, zucchini, beans, onions, anchovies, pineapple, and

bean

onion

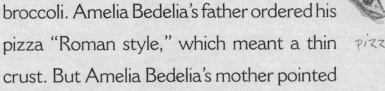
pizza

olive

broccoli. Amelia Bedelia's father ordered his pizza "Roman style," which meant a thin crust. But Amelia Bedelia's mother pointed out that the crust would break under the weight of his toppings. Amelia Bedelia and Audrey stuck with just extra cheese.

mushroom

pineapple

A pitcher of lemonade arrived, and Doc proposed a toast.

"Here's to fishing *and* catching," he said. "May you do both!"

broccoli

"To our fisher girls, Amelia Bedelia and Audrey!" said Amelia Bedelia's mother.

There was enough pizza left over to fill a whole box, which they took home for tomorrow's lunch.

Zucchini

pepperoni

green pepper

Chapter 12

Stumped

On the day of the contest, Lake Largemouth was swarming with boats. Doc and Amelia Bedelia's dad took off in the mayor's speedboat to try their luck. Later, Amelia Bedelia's mother and Mrs. Doc headed into town to shop. Before they left, Amelia Bedelia's mother gave her daughter a hug.

"Have fun," she said. "We'll be rooting for you. Take this leftover pizza with you for lunch."

Audrey was unusually grumpy when she picked up Amelia Bedelia in the boat. She banged into the dock and dropped her spare reel overboard.

"Is something wrong, Stinky?" asked Amelia Bedelia.

"I'm doomed," said Audrey. "Grandma Doc accidentally washed my lucky fishing shirt. Now it isn't lucky anymore."

Amelia Bedelia inhaled deeply. Yes, that amazing aroma that had hung over Audrey in the boat was gone. "But you're really good at fishing," she said. "You don't need luck." She stepped into the boat and sat on her favorite perch.

"Fishing is mostly luck," said Audrey.

They headed out full speed ahead, but they didn't get very far.

BANG!

BANG!

The engine conked out.

"Oh, no!" said Audrey. "Was that what I think it was?"

That's when Amelia Bedelia remembered the stump that Doc had warned them about.

"I can't believe this is happening," said Audrey. She tried to start the engine, but it was dead. She was close to tears. "I planned for everything. Oh, why did Grandma Doc have to wash my shirt?"

"We have oars," said Amelia Bedelia. "We can row."

"But it'll take so long," said Audrey. "The contest will be over before we get to my spot."

Amelia Bedelia felt terrible. She should have remembered about that stump. If she could have kicked herself, she would have kicked herself.

Amelia Bedelia thought for a minute. "I know," she said. "Let's fish right here."

"There's nothing here," said Audrey.

"Unless you want to catch that stupid stump!"

"But Stinky," Amelia Bedelia said, "didn't you tell me that bass like to hang out by tree roots? A stump that big must have hundreds of roots. There could be a big bass waiting down there."

Audrey wiped her eyes. "It's worth a try, I guess," she said.

She picked up her rod and cast her favorite lure near the underwater stump. But her lure got snagged so badly that she had to break it off. The same thing happened with her second-favorite lure. When she lost her third-favorite lure and got her reel tangled, Audrey quit.

Amelia Bedelia was out of

ideas. Her stomach growled. She opened the pizza box. She offered a slice to Audrey, but Audrey was so angry that she took the slice of pizza and flung it as hard as she could. It skipped across the surface like a flat stone until it came to rest right above the stump.

That piece of pizza floated like an abandoned ship. Suddenly, a whirlpool opened beneath it and inhaled the pizza.

Amelia Bedelia and Audrey looked at each other. "What was *that*?" they both yelled.

"That," said Audrey, "was a ginormous bigmouth bass." Her eyes lit up, and she grabbed her rod. "Oh, no!" she said. "I'll never untangle this reel in time!"

Amelia Bedelia picked up her cane pole. "Try this," she said.

Amelia Bedelia sprinkled some water from the lake onto the last piece of pizza, to soften it. This slice had a crazy combination of toppings.

"I hope Mr. Bass likes anchovies," said Audrey, as she carefully squished the pizza around the hook, forming a lump as big as a tennis ball. "You cast it, Soaky,"

she said. "You've practiced it all week."

"Okay," said Amelia Bedelia. "But then I'm handing it to you."

Amelia Bedelia looked at the lake. Ripples were still moving out across the water. She imagined a giant bull's-eye. The center was where their pizza ball had to land. She leaned back, yelled,

PIZZA PIE!

and cast the bait dead center with a *SPLASH*! She handed the pole to Audrey. Nothing happened. Seconds passed. Still nothing. More nothing.

And then . . . nothing at all.

When they looked at each other, *then* it happened. It was like a toilet had flushed in the lake. The pizza disappeared into the biggest mouth Amelia Bedelia had ever seen on a fish. Audrey let the fish take the dough ball to the bottom. Then she leaned back hard to set the hook and snag the fish.

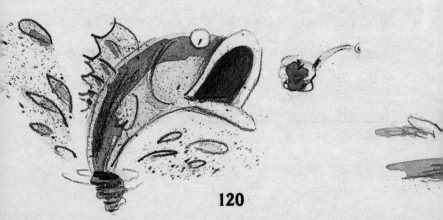

"Did you get it?" asked Amelia Bedelia.

"I think so," said Audrey.

She had, because just then the only thing that kept Audrey from being yanked overboard was Amelia Bedelia, holding her tightly around her waist. The fish circled their boat one way, then the other. The fish went right. The fish went left, then jumped in the air, walking across the surface on its tail. Luckily,

that bass tired out before they did.

"Grab the cooler!" yelled Audrey.

"How can you be thirsty at a time like this?" asked Amelia Bedelia.

"Empty it and put it in the lake," said Audrey. Amelia Bedelia held the cooler overboard and let it fill with lake water. Then Audrey steered the fish into the cooler to trap it. The cooler was big, but the fish was huge. It barely fit. "One, two, three, *lift*!" said Audrey. They heaved the cooler full of water and fish into the boat. Water sloshed and the fish flapped, but

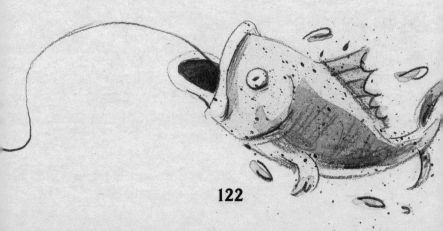

they did it, and then they collapsed into giggles.

Suddenly Amelia Bedelia remembered the symbols of the boat and the fish on their map. This fish was almost as big as the boat. Her fortune had come true!

"ZZZZRRRRR ENTRIES GZZZ PRIZE ZZ FISH ZZ TEN MINUTES!"

The staticky loudspeaker on the public dock told them that they were running out of time.

"Hurry, Soaky!" shouted Audrey.

They took turns rowing and holding the top on the cooler until they got to the public dock.

"We were getting worried about you two," said Doc. "Hurry, it's almost over!"

"Dad, help us!" shouted Amelia Bedelia as they struggled with the cooler.

Amelia Bedelia's father and Doc each grabbed a handle and hoisted it onto the dock. "Whew!" said Doc. "What's in here?"

"Five hundred dollars!" said Amelia Bedelia.

Chapter 13

Miss REALLY Bigmouth

Audrey and Amelia Bedelia threaded their way through the crowd with the help of Doc yelling "Gangway!" and "Coming through!" At last they arrived in front of the very official-looking judges, a big scale, and a tape measure on a table.

The newly crowned Miss Bigmouth stood beside them, shimmering like a mermaid in a sparkly green cape and tiara.

"Okay, young ladies," said one of the judges. "You're in just under the wire."

Amelia Bedelia looked up. She saw balloons shaped like fish, but no wires.

The girls lifted the cooler lid together.

"Whoa-ho-ho. . . ," sputtered Doc.

Amelia Bedelia's father just opened and closed his mouth like a fish himself, but no words came out. A hush fell over the crowd.

"Hold up your lunker, ladies, and let everyone have a look," said a judge.

Audrey took the head, Amelia Bedelia grabbed the tail, and on the count of three, they hoisted their fish up in the air. The crowd gasped. So did the judges.

A photographer started snapping pictures for the paper. Her camera made annoying little flashes right before the big flash. Those flashes always made Amelia Bedelia close her eyes—and that's what she did. But since a bass has no eyelids, the flashes startled him back to life. He flicked his tail hard and soared up, up, up into the air.

"Grab him!" yelled Amelia Bedelia.

"Come back here!" yelled Audrey.

And come back he did, landing right on top of Miss Bigmouth's head. Her tiara popped up and came to rest on the head of that monster bass, crowning him King of the Bigmouths.

That's when Miss Bigmouth gasped, then let out a scream heard clear across the lake. She dove into the water. King Bigmouth landed with a big, splashy *plop* and swam away for freedom, crown and all.

Although absolutely everyone agreed that Amelia Bedelia and Audrey's fish had been the winner, it had never been officially weighed or measured. So the judges had to declare another winner.

The lucky fisherman thanked the judges, shook their hands, and then signed the prize check over to Amelia Bedelia and Audrey.

The next morning, Amelia Bedelia's dad packed up the car to go back home. Doc, Mrs. Doc, and Audrey came over to say good-bye.

"Soaky!" yelled Audrey. "Look at this!"

She held up a copy of the *Lake Largemouth News*. On the front page was a

BIGMOUTH

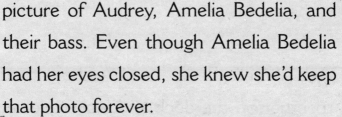

picture of Audrey, Amelia Bedelia, and their bass. Even though Amelia Bedelia had her eyes closed, she knew she'd keep that photo forever.

They all had a good laugh, but even so, the morning was a sad one. Amelia Bedelia's mother baked blueberry muffins for Doc and wrote down the recipe for her easy-breezy appetizer for Mrs. Doc. Amelia Bedelia had picked a bunch of

wildflowers for Audrey, and the girls arranged them in a pretty purple vase. Amelia Bedelia's dad fixed the leaky faucets in the cabin so that when the mayor's family came to stay, they could spend the whole time relaxing instead of working. Plus, he topped off the gas tank in their boat.

As the grown-ups said their good-byes, Amelia Bedelia and Audrey stood together on the dock and looked out at Lake Largemouth one last time.

"Do you think our bass is back home at the stump?" asked Audrey.

"Yup," said Amelia Bedelia. "He's wearing that tiara and ordering pizza."

The thought of that made them both

burst out laughing until they cried.

"Amelia Bedelia," said Audrey, "I wish I had a sister just like you."

"I was thinking the same thing," said Amelia Bedelia. "You'd be a great big sister."

They hugged one last long, hard hug, and then Amelia Bedelia climbed into the car. She lowered her window and yelled, "Smell you later, Stinky!"

"Stay dry, Soaky!" shouted Audrey.

The cabin and Lake Largemouth disappeared in a cloud of dust as Amelia Bedelia's family drove off.

Chapter 14

Roam, Sweet Home

The drive home was very different. There was no more roaming. There was no more getting lost. They got on the highway and zoomed.

The road was smooth, so Amelia Bedelia worked on her journal. It was her longest entry yet. She wrote down everything she was thinking about

Audrey and Lake Largemouth and catching the biggest bigmouth.

After a while, Amelia Bedelia's father looked at her in the rearview mirror and asked, "How big was your fish?"

Amelia Bedelia held up her hands to show him. Then she made it a bit bigger.

Amelia Bedelia's mother smiled. "Like father, like daughter," she said. "Sweetie, you look tired. Try forty winks."

Amelia Bedelia *was* tired. She tried blinking her eyes forty times, but that only made her feel more tired. She got up to thirty-three winks before she dozed off. When she woke up, her mom was driving past the POP. sign for their town. Amelia Bedelia's crayon marks had washed away.

That's okay, she thought. The population was right again, now that they were back.

They stopped at the Paw Palace to pick up Finally (who wiggled and wagged and kissed Amelia Bedelia again and again), then headed to their house. They turned into their driveway, and Amelia Bedelia felt the car go *bump-bump* over the uneven sidewalk. That's when she knew she was home at last.

"Wow," said Amelia Bedelia's father, pointing at the odometer. "Look at that. We drove five hundred and two miles exactly."

ODO
502 MI

"Next time," said Amelia Bedelia, "let's roam for a thousand miles, like Mom's fortune!"

"That's the spirit," said her father.

"You two can go, just send me a postcard," said her mother, turning off the car.

The daisies that had been in full bloom when they left were now gone, all but one. Amelia Bedelia's mother picked it.

"Welcome home, honey," she said to Amelia Bedelia's dad. "That was fun."

"Same time next year?" he asked.

"Yay!" yelled Amelia Bedelia.

Amelia Bedelia's mother tucked the daisy behind her ear and smiled.

Amelia Bedelia raced around the house making sure everything was there. She ran into her room. Her dolls and stuffed animals stared back at her. They looked surprised to see her. Yet something was different. Something had changed. She glanced at herself in her mirror.

Her hair was a little bit longer. She'd grown a teensy bit taller. More freckles had bloomed across her nose to keep the others company. But that wasn't it. When she looked into her own eyes, she realized that *she* was what had changed. She had taken this trip and would never

be the same. The Amelia Bedelia who had left a week ago was not the Amelia Bedelia who had returned.

That night, Amelia Bedelia took her journal out of her backpack. Thumbing through it, she could recall their whole vacation—the boring and fun and frustrating and fantastic parts. It was all there, waiting for her. She taped in the picture of Audrey and her and their fish. Then she remembered her father's fortune—the one from the Chinese restaurant. Now she had the perfect spot for it. She taped it to the top of the page.

Amelia Bedelia read the fortune out loud: "'Follow your dreams.'" Then she wrote her shortest entry of all.

Amelia Bedelia turned out her light and went to sleep, to work on her own dreams.

Read all these great books
about Amelia Bedelia!

Amelia Bedelia Means Business

#1

a Parish   pictures by Lynne Avril

Amelia Bedelia Unleashed

#2

by Herman Parish   pictures by Lynne Avril

#1

Amelia Bedelia Road Trip!

WRONG WAY
ADVENTURE
RIGHT WAY

#3

Amelia
Bedelia

Hi!
Turn the page
for a special
sneak peek
at my next
adventure!

#4

Amelia Bedelia Goes Wild!

by Herman Parish   pictures by Lynne Avril

Coming soon!

Chapter 1

Sick as a Dog

Amelia Bedelia was sick. She was really, really, really, really, *really* sick. She was sick of being her bedroom. She was sick of rearranging her plush animals and dolls. Sick of gazing out the window at the beautiful spring day. Sick of thinking about how much fun her friends were having on the class field trip to the zoo.

Most of all, she was sick of being sick.

"How's the worst patient in the world?" asked Amelia Bedelia's mother. She put a bowl of soup and a grilled cheese sandwich on Amelia Bedelia's desk.

Amelia Bedelia stood up on her bed.

"I'm all better now!" she announced. To prove it, she began jumping up and down and waving her arms around. Quickly she plopped back down again.

"Mommy," she said. "Make the room stop spinning!"

"Don't make yourself dizzy, sweetie," her mother said, tucking her back in. "I don't want you to fall and hit your head, on top of having the flu."

Amelia Bedelia began coughing. She had been coughing and sneezing all day long. It took all her strength just to toss her used tissues into the trash can.

"Are you okay?" asked her mother. "The pesky flu bug is tough."

"The flu is an insect?" asked Amelia Bedelia. "This isn't fair! How can a little insect make me miss seeing all the cool animals at the zoo?"

Two Ways to Say It

By Amelia Bedelia

"Get your feet wet."   "Try something new!"

"Let's go buy some staples."   "Let's buy the basic items we really need."

"This is a one-horse town."   "This town is tiny!"

"There's a lot to see in our own backyard."   "We don't have to go far to see new and interesting things."

"I'll show you the ropes."   "I'll show you how to do it."

"Catch forty winks."   "Take a nap."